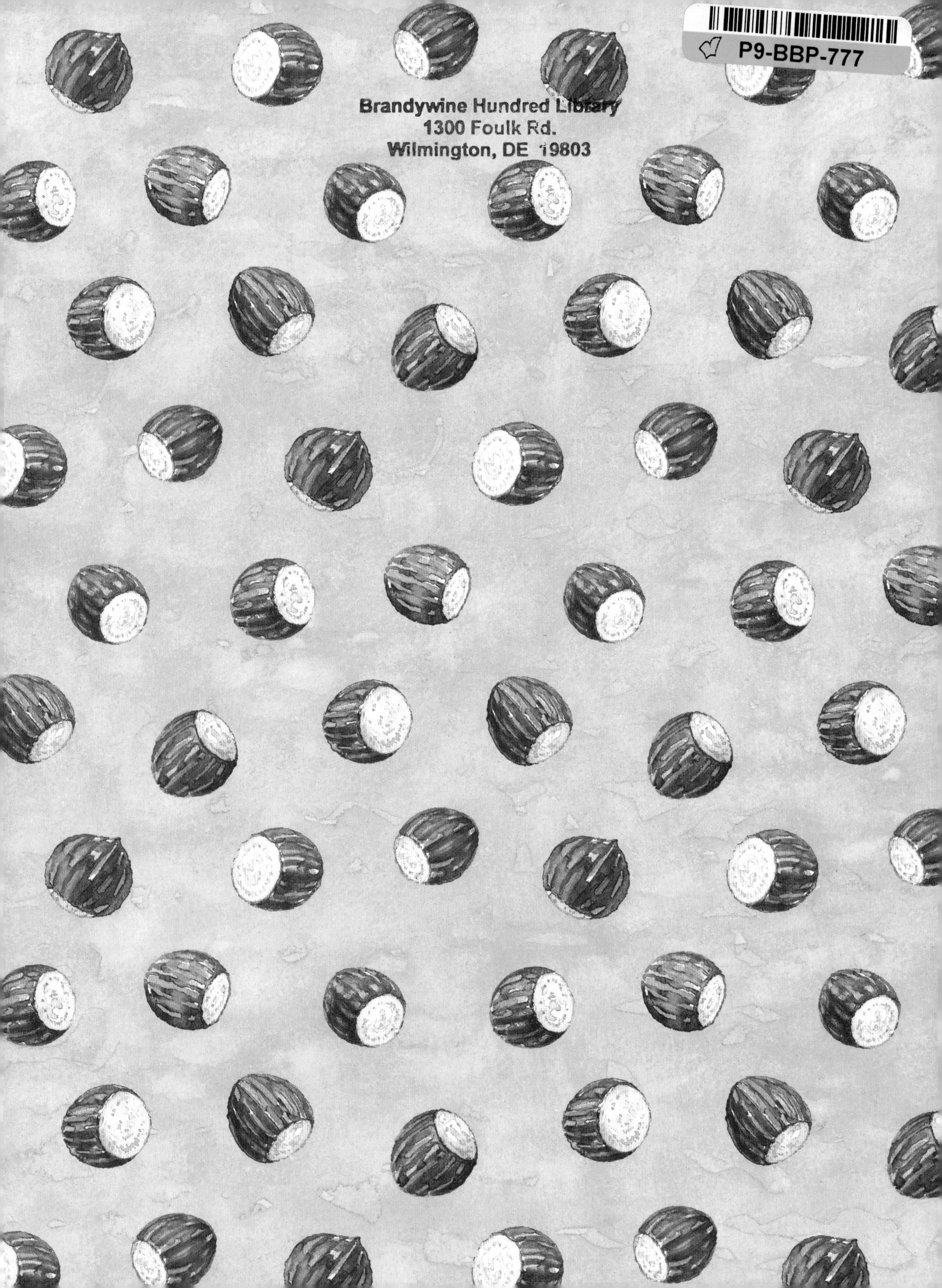

MARCUS PFISTER was born in Bern, Switzerland. After studying at the Art School of Bern, he apprenticed as a graphic designer and worked in an advertising agency before becoming self-employed in 1984. His debut picture book, "The Sleepy Owl", was published by NorthSouth in 1986, but his big breakthrough came six years later with "The Rainbow Fish". Today, Marcus has illustrated over fifty books that have been translated into more than fifty languages and received countless international awards. He lives with his wife, Debora, and his children in Bern.

First published in Switzerland under the title *Wer hat die Haselnuss geklaut? Eine Räubergeschichte.*

Translated by David Henry Wilson.

First published in the United States, Great Britain, Canada, Australia, and New Zealand in 2019 by NorthSouth Books Inc., an imprint of NordSüd Verlag AG, CH-8050 Zürich, Switzerland.

Distributed in the United States by NorthSouth Books Inc., New York 10016.
Library of Congress Cataloging-in-Publication Data is available.
Printed in Latvia
ISBN: 978-0-7358-4382-0
1 3 5 7 9 · 10 8 6 4 2

www.northsouth.com
www.rainbowfish.us
Meet Marcus Pfister at www.marcuspfister.ch

MARCUS PFISTER

WHO STOLE THE HAZELNUTS?

A FOREST MYSTERY

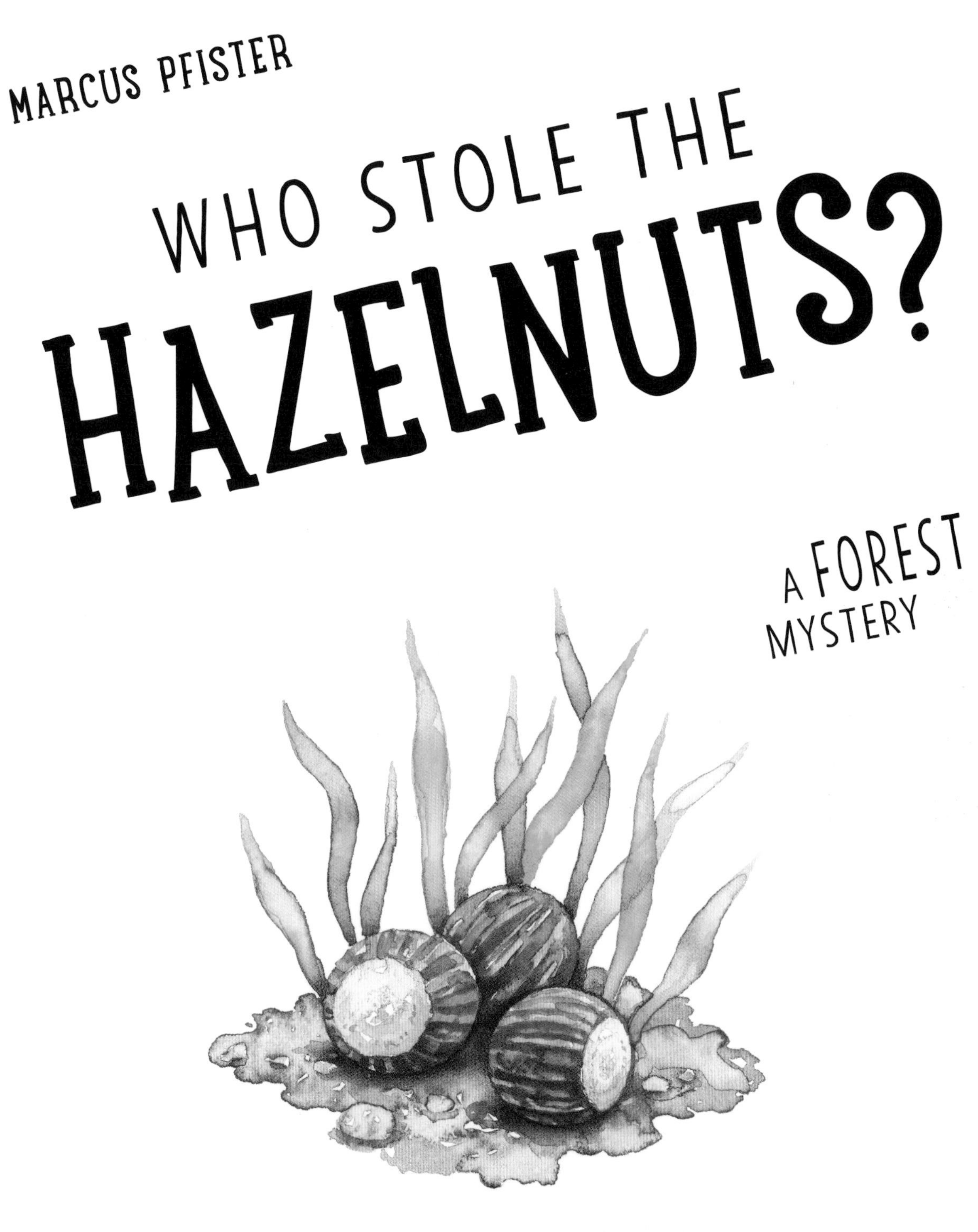

TRANSLATED BY DAVID HENRY WILSON

All was quiet and all was still,

Until there came a scream so shrill
That all the trees quaked and quivered,
And all the animals shook and shivered.
The voice shrieked, "This is what I feared!
My hazelnuts have disappeared!

"All three have vanished. Not a trace.
Stolen from their hiding place.
Oh, such a crime's beyond belief!
Help, oh help me find the thief!"
But who had caused him such distress?
The squirrel simply couldn't guess.

The squirrel went to see the mole,
Who'd built a hill, not dug a hole.
"This hill," he thought, "would be just right
To keep my hazels out of sight."

“A thief,” the mole said, “there may be,
But I know for a fact it isn’t me.”

The squirrel went to see the mouse.
No doubt in that tiny house
He'd find the nuts and find the thief,
And that would be a great relief.

"A thief," the mouse said, "you may see,
But I know for a fact it isn't me."

Next, the squirrel accused the rabbit
Of practicing a sneaky habit . . . .
"You took my nuts!" the squirrel protested.
"Give them back or you'll be arrested!"

"Arrest me!" said the bunny. "I'll soon be free,
As I know for a fact it isn't me."

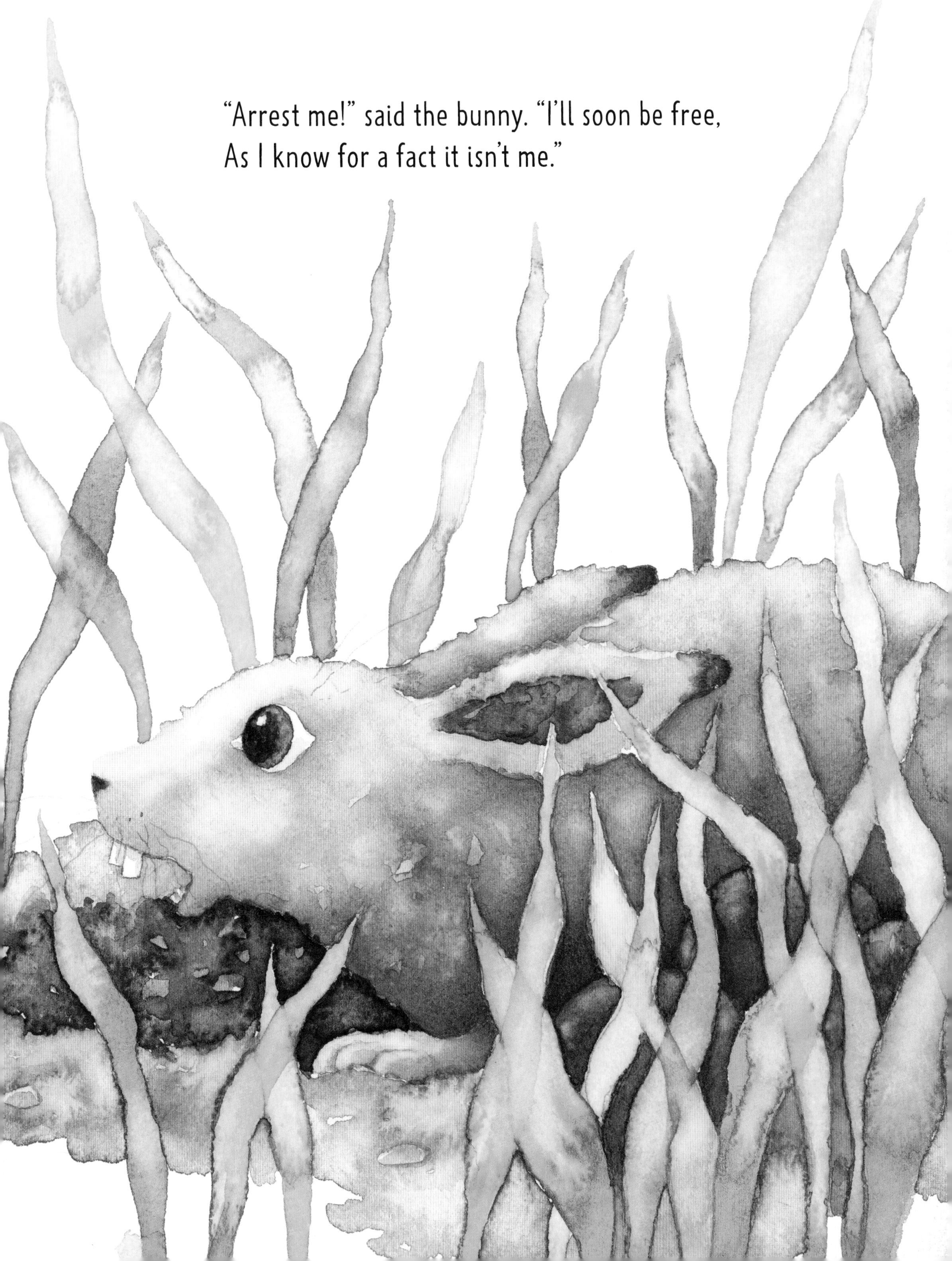

"Perhaps the hamster's the guilty beast.
Any food for him's a feast.
His chubby hamster cheeks could hide
Three nuts and plenty more besides."

"Thief?" said the hamster. "How wrong can you be?
I know for a fact it isn't me."

The squirrel left, full of frustration,
Then met the fox. Same accusation:
"You stole my nuts!" The fox just laughed.
"Me, steal nuts? Don't be so daft.
Chickens I'll steal. Lovely to chew.
Stay around, and I'll chew you too."

The squirrel sadly went home to his tree.
Where, oh where could the lost nuts be?
His hungry tummy started rumbling.
He needed nuts to stop it grumbling.
But you can't eat something that isn't there.
He shed a tear of sheer despair.

But wait! What's that among the leaves?
Three nuts? THREE NUTS? There were no thieves!
He'd gone round searching everywhere,
But only he could have put them there.
For all this fuss he was to blame.
He could have hung his head in shame.

Instead, he cried in his loudest voice,
"I've found my nuts! Rejoice! Rejoice!"
The others had a different feeling:
He'd accused them all of stealing!

"Next time you want to make a fuss,
Accuse yourself instead of us!"

The squirrel realized what he'd done,
And apologized to everyone.
Now it was well past time for tea,
So he cracked the nutshells one, two, three,
Tasted them—nothing suspicious—
Then ate them all. They were delicious!